For Walt

DEADLY GAME AT STONY CREEK

DEADLY GAME AT STONY CREEK

Peter Zachary Cohen

pictures by MICHAEL J. DEAS

THE DIAL PRESS · NEW YORK

Published by The Dial Press
1 Dag Hammarskjold Plaza, New York, New York 10017

Printed in the United States of America First Printing
Design by Denise Cronin Neary

Library of Congress Cataloging in Publication Data
Cohen, Peter Zachary. Deadly game at Stony Creek.
Summary: A pack of wild killer dogs
is hunted down by two teen-age boys.
[1. Dogs—Fiction. 2. Hunting—Fiction]
I. Deas, Michael. II. Title.
PZ7.C663De [Fic] 78-51772
ISBN 0-8037-1816-0 ISBN 0-8037-1817-9 lib. bdg.

DEADLY GAME AT STONY CREEK

In the damp shadows of a thick woods twenty miles from town, five large hungry dogs were following a path a goat had walked. A horse passed there too, but it was the scent of the goat that might mean food.

At the same time, in town, there was a loud *crick,* like the sound of a snapping twig, from the clock high on the ninth-grade homeroom wall. It was one minute to twelve and a lot of kids were looking up at that clock. But Cliff Brookings felt the clock was looking back only at him. Surely no one felt closer than he to that clock. For nine months he'd watched it hesitate, then suddenly snap away another minute, and another and another, like a squirrel high in a tree somewhere slowly but steadily cracking nuts. And steadily, minute by minute, together they'd brought the summer back.

Steadily, Cliff thought, one throw at a time, he could get to the major leagues.

Crick. The clock's hands came together as if in prayer. Noon. The buzzer sounded and the building filled with the rumble of feet hurrying for the exits. Vacation had begun.

Cliff took his time. The bus would wait a little, and he was not all that eager to reach it.

In the hallway Len Swanson, coming from the tenth-grade room, slowed up to talk. "You figured how to make Town League practice this summer?" he started in.

Cliff wanted to shout, "Yes!" but he had to shake his head. "We still live twenty-five miles out, you know."

Len screwed up his face as if in pain. Baseball meant as much to him as it did to Cliff. "Man, you can't let that stop you. Haven't you been working on your old man?"

"Mostly I've been working *for* him."

"Yeah, great. Too bad you couldn't have held 'em in town just another couple of years."

Cliff shrugged. There was no point in going into that again.

"Holman's going to be coaching again, you know," Len went on. "He still won't let you play unless you come in for practice."

From anyone else such egging would have been annoying. But Cliff had played with Len for two of their three years in Peewee League when Cliff had lived in town, and he knew Len wanted to make it to the big leagues as badly as he did.

"I'll practice at home," Cliff said resignedly. "Just like I did last summer."

"Just like you didn't play last summer either."

"Holman doesn't coach Legion ball," Cliff countered. "When I'm old enough for that next year I'll be old enough to drive. I can bring myself in then."

They stepped outside and the bright sunshine made both of them squint and turn their heads a little.

The big pale gray dog in the lead stayed hidden in the brush for a ways, then hurriedly crossed the path to make certain the scent was still there. He continued in his low crouching walk through the brush on the other side of the path till he realized he was coming to the end of the woods. The scent of pasture grass became strong, and bright sunlight shone through the trees.

Len walked awkwardly, his arms loaded with all the stuff he was taking home, but his voice continued steadily, "You'll still have to make the Legion team, Cliff. And you'll never make it if you don't get to practice in real games now, with real live people hitting the ball, and real guys on the bases trying to steal, and lots of eyes watching you."

Cliff's temper was starting to ignite. Those were worries he'd been trying to fight off almost constantly for two years. He didn't need Len or anyone else hammering them at him. He shifted his own load of school stuff and said, "I've got my own eyes watching me."

"That's not enough." Len spoke calmly, like an older brother sure of having the last word.

"I bet I get more practice at home alone than you get here with all the horseplay from guys like Hal and Barney," Cliff snapped back at him. "And I'd rather face those wild dogs out there than get yelled at for everything, the way Holman coaches."

Len shrugged. "Holman's jazz doesn't bother me,

just as long as I get to play." His pale-blue eyes looked directly at Cliff. "If you want to get good enough to make the Legion team where some scout can see you, you'd better start getting into prac—"

Beside the walk was a thick stand of lilac bushes, full of large clusters of sweet-smelling purple flowers. A step beyond the bushes a path from the grade school met the sidewalk, and from behind the lilacs Karla Dobley hobbled out in front of them. They stopped abruptly to let her pass.

"Hi, Karla," Cliff said. He couldn't keep from staring, so he had to say something. And he heard Len say the same. But the words were pretty lame and Cliff couldn't help feeling foolish and rude. How many fourth graders did he naturally say hi to?

"Hello," Karla murmured, and kept on going. The new, white bandages on her leg were thinner than the other ones had been. Fresh purple scars showed between the pads that remained. It was hard to act natural close to someone who'd been torn up by wild dogs, who'd been right at death but hadn't died, yet who might start dying at any moment. They'd all heard that rabies injections didn't always work. They'd heard too that rabies could live in her body for years, striking her at any time. What could you say to someone who had to live with that? Cliff forgot everything else for a moment and just watched and wondered what it was like for her, and what it would be like for him.

What would it be like clinging to a tree branch, feeling hard teeth tearing your leg, trying to pull you down?

What would it be like to escape and find that your leg would never straighten right? That you could never really run or throw or field again? Never.

Cliff tore his eyes away from Karla and met Len's eyes turning back to him.

"Well, there's worse things than missing some practices," Cliff said softly. He started to walk toward his bus again, feeling a chilled and grateful relief at how smoothly he could walk.

"That's for sure," Len murmured. "Just make certain that wild pack out there doesn't grab you."

"You bet," said Cliff.

The lead dog was moving much more slowly. His tail drooped between his hind legs. The other four dogs crept up beside him. Two of them were tall and long, with short brown hair, and so naturally skinny that their hunger showed only in the dark hollows around their eyes. They were almost identical, except that one had noticeably lighter-colored ears. A shaggy red female padded carefully behind those two, and a black dog with bony shoulders and knobby white hips moved anxiously but quietly behind her. They all eased into a grove of saplings, and there was the goat.

As usual Cliff took a seat in the middle, by himself, and soon enough the bus started. It swung right at the hospital corner and headed toward the city park on its way out of town. High overhead a flock of crows went past, all spread out, going faster than the bus was yet moving. Because snowy weather had lasted so long into spring, they were late arriving from the south and seemed intent on losing no more time. The beating of their dark wings caught Cliff's eye and he was reminded of a country saying: "Keep an eye out for crows. They seem to gather where there's danger." Crows had raised a ruckus over the woods last spring when Chris Erickson and a friend from town had gone skating and broken through the rotting ice. There were more ways to get killed than by wild dogs, Cliff thought.

But there was little danger here. The bus was passing between the city waterworks on one side and the park on the other. Cliff stared out at the two ball fields—empty now, but they'd be filled with kids out playing baseball right after lunch. Cliff longed to stop, but the bus kept right on going.

The crows flew on, dodging around the smokestack of the Hoppley North Plywood Mill. Beneath them the dry firm ground rumpled into low hills and became crowded with trees, interrupted by lakes that were still high with melted snow. Even the boggy sloughs glistened full from edge to edge. Only from the height of a flying crow could one see which waters were shallow and thick with grass and which were deep. Small pastures opened amidst the trees, some still full of bulldozed timber, others with only sawed stumps. There were some fields deep brown from recent plowing, others green from earlier planting. But mostly there were broad patches of solid-green forest.

The bus stopped at the railroad spur that led toward the Mill, then picked up speed again. More shade than sunlight was coming in through the windows as the woods sliding by outside grew thicker. Cliff heard the familiar spraying rattle adding to the bus's hum and rumble as it left the pavement and continued along the sandy gravel road. The crows flew on. They were not tired and nothing attracted their fancy.

2 «

The gray dog's front legs were as thick as the saplings that were now all around him.

Four years ago, and far to the south, he'd grown larger than anyone had expected. He'd begun to defend his small backyard in town more fiercely than anyone wanted. His size had made breaking into neighborhood garbage cans mere play, and the annoyance of being constantly tied had started him snapping even at people he knew. No one else would take him, so he was taken on a long ride in the back of a car and dumped out along a country road in the middle of the night.

He'd chased after the car until he was exhausted. Hunger had drawn him to the door of a farmhouse, then later to another, then a third. But snarling dogs on their home ground and the narrowly missing blast of a shotgun had kept him moving.

He'd learned alone to hunt quietly and patiently, then leap and snap hard, without hesitation, whether on open prairie or in a farmyard at night. And he'd learned to run for new territory the moment he realized that men were hunting for him.

More than a year ago he'd run off the prairies into the dense woods of the lake country. Now this spring the sides of his hungry body were very thin. His thick gray fur no longer lay smoothly. He looked like a pile of old wood shavings, a pile that kept creeping forward among the saplings.

He held his blunt head low, still sniffing and listening. His eyes were like two polished brown stones that didn't move as he kept watching the white goat.

The goat had begun to jump about in the center of the clearing. All day yesterday she had been led behind a horse until she could barely walk another step. Goat scent had been spread far through the woods. Now that she was rested again, the goat

couldn't move more than seven or eight steps before being stopped by a chain, and she was restless.

The goat leaped harder, almost straight up, and was tugged down by the chain. She stumbled along off balance for several steps with one foreleg dragging beneath her like a bird with a broken wing.

The gray dog shivered with eagerness, his sharp hunger stinging. But he had hunted at this clearing before, he knew what leashes were, and he had never seen a leashed animal off by itself this way. He had learned to beware of the unusual. He stayed crouched on the soft earth, his tail flat between his hind legs. He knew the goat could not escape. He would lie quietly and wait until dark.

Then he looked quickly to his side as he sensed a different movement. The two long-legged brown dogs were standing, staring at the goat, as rigid as dark and rotting limbs in the shadows. Both were more inclined to chase than hunt; they were confused unless something fled, and the goat wasn't running away. They were waiting for the gray dog's quick decisions and sure movements to solve their own confusion.

Close behind them the reddish female was sitting. She made no more movement than a shaggy stump.

It was the stocky dog beyond her who was starting to fidget. Like the female he'd been a farm dog—

until a night late last summer when he'd rushed out at the wild ones and decided to join instead of fight. Now he stayed with them for their company, and because the business of hunting his own food had stirred up exciting instincts. He was hungry and impatient, and getting more and more excited. He watched the uneasy goat make two more jerked-short jumps. That movement meant food. The goat's awkwardness meant it was wounded, easily caught. The stocky dog's mouth opened and closed. His tongue stretched forward and back between his teeth.

At the same time, on a deer-hunting platform built high in a large tree directly across the clearing, a man sat quietly, his rifle leaning against the trunk beside him. He had been there for hours. He sighed deeply and tried to stretch without moving too much. He watched the restless goat and tried to be patient. Next to him another man held his gun across his lap and stared intently down. He was Karla Dobley's father, and in his mind he could still hear Karla screaming from the apple trees where she'd gone to look for straying hens. He'd had no time to get a gun then. He'd raced his tractor at full throttle across the garden and through a wooden fence to chase the dogs off before they killed her.

But they'd torn her leg and stiffened and scarred it, and she could die yet if any of them was rabid.

Hidden in the shadows of the saplings the gray dog stared with stony brown eyes at the fidgeting movements of the stocky dog and growled in a low, angry rumble. The growl startled the female, and the other dogs quickened their breathing.

The stocky black-and-white dog had gotten so restless he didn't even notice the warning. He saw the goat make another leap and get snapped down harder than before, looking more crippled, more available. The stocky dog charged out from the shadows into the full glare of the sunlight.

His rush startled the red female even more, and she automatically bounded forward too. She almost stopped after just three jumps, but as she passed the brown dogs the one with the paler ears sprang into a dash, intent on not losing his share of the kill. That made the female keep running. Then the gray dog and the other brown dog went leaping for the goat too.

The pale-eared brown dog dashed past the stocky dog into the lead, but the panicked goat leaped and dodged and he went skidding by. Then the stocky dog arrived, grabbing for the nearest thing that moved, the goat's hind feet. He got kicked twice in the face and several of his teeth were broken. The gray dog and the dark-eared brown dog, with more killing sense, drove at the goat's neck and tore it open with rapid slashes. At the same time the female grabbed a flank. She tasted the goat's warm blood. The smell of food filled her head. There was a loud noise as something smashed her away from the goat and sprawled her on the ground. She tried to get back to the food but couldn't move, and died in the midst of her silent struggle.

Meanwhile the stocky dog, his mouth dripping his own blood, had snatched at the other flank. Another roar. He leaped as the goat had leaped, then fell awkwardly, crippled, his legs scraping behind him in the grass, slower, and slower.

More quick shots followed, but the gray dog and both brown dogs had reacted instantly, darting swiftly away through the grass. Poor targets.

They got away from the clearing unscratched and started to escape deeper among the trees, but had to stop. More shots filled the woods. Other volunteers were now hurrying into action, spreading out through the woods, shooting guns into the air, creating a ring of noise intended to drive the dogs into a wide slough that spread out at the narrow end of the clearing. There'd be no hiding places that way, no solid ground to run on, and they could be killed.

The gray dog spun about and led the others through the woods directly toward the slough. He'd hunted frogs there several times. Guided by his memory and his nose, quickly scenting the difference between bottomless muck and the firmer clumps of root-bound mud, he was able to leap steadily from soggy clump to soggy clump. The brown dogs, better jumpers than he, followed closely.

They crossed the slough before the ring of hunters could close around them, before the men even knew they were gone. They ran up a brushy hill and through more woods, quiet woods except for their own crackling rush. Then they ran downslope and came to a road.

The open roadway looked as dangerous to cross as the clearing had been. The gray dog was aware that now only two dogs were following him. He continued on beside the road, splashing along in a ditch at a tired but urgent trot. His tufted ears sensed the approaching hum of a motor. Though weary, and weakened by lack of food, he began to run again. He felt he had to get beyond the road for the same reason he'd had to cross the slough. He ran tiredly as hard as he could, trying to reach a small creek that he knew went into a culvert through which they could cross the road underneath and out of sight.

3 «

Cliff moved restlessly about on the bus seat. Even with his ball glove and a year's notebooks and folders beside him, he felt how much spare room he had and was reminded that in baseball he would have to depend more on skill and speed than size. Yet he felt exercised and limber, and he wished he could get out in a ball park again and see what he could do.

It had been two years since his dad's promotion from Supply Chief to Assistant Director at the Mill had made purchase of the farm possible. Since then the school bus had been his only way of getting home. Dad's job had put him on the road a lot, at least for the next few years. His mom had taken on a Fleetwell Home Products sales route. It helped pay the mortgage but it kept her away too. The daily farm chores were Cliff's responsibility. He couldn't blame his parents, even when he tried to. The farm was something they had wanted for a long time, and if they'd waited, the price of land would only have gone higher. And Cliff knew what it was like to want something badly.

The bus swayed over the familiar hills and around the sloughs, making short dashes down straight roads through the woods, where crop fields and pastures opened suddenly among the trees, then sailed behind as the trees closed in. He knew they'd covered nine and a half miles when they stopped at the Rabens'. It was two more miles to the Dornes', another four to the Ericksons'. Rick, whose brother had drowned last spring along the shore of Two Moon Lake while the crows had raised a ruckus overhead, got off there. Almost every trip Cliff thought about that. Not so much about the crows as about the way things could trip you, catch you, stop you from getting where you wanted to go.

Once, with his mind on statistics, he'd figured

that he rode this bus twice a day, 180 days each year, 25 miles directly out from town in the afternoon, and 35 miles around going in in the morning—60 miles each day. 10,800 miles a year. Times two years now: 21,600 miles. Almost around the earth. And still he'd gone nowhere. That's how it felt. In spite of his not wanting it to, that's how it felt going back again to practice all summer alone, in the same way every day, throwing against the same stone wall. Hitting the same swinging ball.

The Peewee League had gotten him started when he'd lived in town, but now he needed the Town League to get enough experience to make the Legion team. He needed the Legion team to put him where a scout could notice him, a big-league scout, a college scout, anybody.

But this bus was taking him nowhere.

To ease the pain of those thoughts he began again to imagine how he would fool all of them next year at the Legion tryouts. There'd be kids from three towns, and most of them wouldn't know him or remember him, because they wouldn't ever have played against him in Town League. He'd come in and show them how snappily he'd learned to play the infield, and especially the hot corner at third base, just by working hard in his own yard out in the country all by himself—just like Dad said.

"A man's got to stand on his own," his dad had told him. "That means learning the basics, doing 'em over and over again. When you go to a Town practice you chase a few balls, swing at a few, and spend most of your time punching the pocket of your mitt, shooting the bull, and waiting. An hour's workout here'll be worth two weeks in town. And you won't have to wait till a field's free. We can do everything, get ready for everything, right here on our own ground. On our own ground we can do things on our own. And when you're ready to drive, you can get back and forth on your own."

Still, he worried about how tough the competition might be, and how confused he might get in the middle of a real game, with guys sliding at him and throwing hard pitches that weren't controlled by a string. Right there in the school bus, just imagining it, he could feel nervous sweat starting to moisten the palms of his hands.

To relax he let his imagination make him already scouted, signed to a contract, and in the minors on a bus taking him to a game. Now his imagination began to soar. He was in the majors, on the Twins maybe—the team didn't really matter—on the bus from the hotel to guard third base—charging bunts, snatching hard-hit balls at the foul line—

Usually he didn't like to imagine himself in the

majors. It seemed too far away, too dangerously braggy. But the dream gave him a freshened feeling of what he wanted for his life, made him more determined to do whatever it took. Besides, this was the last bus ride he could dream on until the end of summer.

He let himself think happy thoughts, losing himself in getting ready to play at third in that major-league game. Then the freckled, pinch-nosed, puffed-cheek face of Eddie Massek rose above the seat in front and looked down at him.

"Off in the glories again?" Eddie guessed and grinned.

Cliff knew that to deny it would make Eddie razz him all the harder. "I'm *planning*," he said strongly. "Don't you ever try planning ahead?"

"That's just what I'm doing now," said Eddie. He'd been one of the first to bounce out of the classroom, down the hall and out the doors, and into the bus. Everywhere Eddie went, he went bouncing. His round face seemed like a smiling ball with a wig of loose hair on it. But he didn't care for sports, so even though they'd been living only a mile apart for two years, they hadn't worked very hard to see each other.

"Why don't we figure on doing some things together this summer?" Eddie's voice kind of bounced too. "Let's start this afternoon. We're closer to each other than to anybody else. And if you ever tried to do things with my sister, you'd be ready for *any*one different."

"Thanks a lot," said Cliff. Cliff had a long bony face, with long smooth hair that curled just a little at his ears. He gave Eddie a long look before he said, "Bring a glove and come on over."

"I wasn't figuring on baseball," said Eddie.

Cliff had guessed that. But whatever they were going to do, Eddie would have to come to his place. "I can't go off when Mom's not home," Cliff told him. "This is her delivery day."

"That's okay. And I bet I can show you some better things than trying to catch one piece of hide with another."

Cliff groaned silently to himself. This could only lead into the same old argument, but he wouldn't back off. He knew what it was he wanted to do, what he *had* to do. Then he remembered how lonely it got, so instead of arguing he tried to be coaxing. "I'll bet you'd be better at it than you think."

Eddie groaned out loud. "But it's just a *game*." Eddie had said that before too, for as long as Cliff could remember.

"So's fishing. So's farming. So's everything a game!" Cliff argued. There seemed no way out of it.

Eddie opened his mouth to speak, but suddenly

from the front seats there was a loud gasp. Then a girl's voice shrieked, "There! It's them! It's them! Hurry!"

Cliff looked first toward the voice. Then, before he could turn the way Karla Dobley was pointing, the bus slowed down abruptly, its brakes squealing as they took hold. Eddie tumbled back into his seat and disappeared. Cliff skidded forward, bumping his chin on the seat back where Eddie's face had been. Then he regained his balance and stared out the window as the bus stopped.

There was a newly planted field below the level of road, with a small but full creek coming out from a culvert under the road and curving along the edge of the field. Cliff saw three dogs, one gray and two dark brown, running along the creek.

"It's them! Keep them away!" He heard Karla crying out, and some of the other girls—he heard Eddie's sister's voice, as bouncy as Eddie's—trying to calm her.

In front of him, Eddie clambered up from the bus floor and leaned toward the window with a painful twist to his face. He was rubbing one elbow.

In the distance the three dogs ran out of sight, down into the darkness of a woods. Cliff had explored enough to know the little creek would lead them into a shallow gulley that opened onto a wide

bog along the shore of Two Moon Lake. He was glad he wasn't exploring in that gulley now.

"Cliff!" Phil Gustav, the driver, had opened the door and gone outside to see better. Now he came jumping back in. "Cliff, we'll get to your place and you start phoning people around here. Get someone to phone the sheriff. Eddie—"

"Yeah!" said Eddie, alert and lively, but sounding a little angry too. He was still holding his elbow.

"Are you on the same phone line as Cliff?"

"Yes," Cliff and Eddie answered together.

"Donna, are you?" Phil asked urgently.

Donna Elrist said no.

"Then you start phoning people west of here. As soon as you get home, both of you! Be sure they know where we saw them!"

Phil ducked into the driver's seat and the bus roared forward. When it stopped by Cliff's mailbox, Cliff left it at a gallop, his arms clamped tightly around his end-of-school load.

"Mom!" He started to give the alarm while he was still just halfway along the drive, running as fast as he could. Bandanna, his dog, came trotting to meet him, furry and black and white, and all of him wriggling in greeting. Cliff didn't slow down and they nearly crashed and fell. He didn't take time to speak to Bandanna. "Mom!"

Mom did not appear. He leaped onto the porch and let the ball glove and books fall to the floor as he whammed open the front door.

"Mom!" he shouted again. "We've seen the dogs!" He ran across the living room, through the kitchen, and two strides out the back door.

"Mom!"

A rooster calmly pecking alongside the shed paid him no attention. He could see the sheep up in the pasture below the raspberry thicket. They seemed unbothered. The car was gone. He remembered it was delivery day.

Cliff ran back inside, went to the cupboard, and yanked it open. Only the .22 and the shotgun were there. The carbine was gone.

Then he looked for a note and found it under the salt shaker as usual:

Cliff—

They've seen the dogs again—think they've got them trapped in a slough by one of Felters' hayfields. I'm delivering that way so am taking the carbine. Take the shotgun to get the sheep in—early. I'll be home by supper. Do chores, and keep gun handy. Stay close to house—in case they're wrong.

Love,
Mom

"They are wrong!" Cliff shouted. He ran to the phone. "Everybody'll be in the wrong place."

He suddenly couldn't remember anybody's number. He nearly dropped the phone book trying to flick its pages too quickly. He started to dial, then realized he'd swung a 3 instead of a 4, so he had to start again. It seemed to be taking so much time. He decided hurriedly that the Ericksons weren't going to answer, and accidentally ripped a page out of the phone book while hurriedly scanning it for another number.

He dialed the Dornes and got their grandmother. He told her what they'd seen from the bus and that she should call the sheriff's office and everyone else she could. He figured she could handle the phoning better than he could. Then he tried to decide what he should do next. He felt nervous sweat in his palms again. This was something he'd never faced before and he didn't know what to do. But with those dogs running around so close by it seemed as if he ought to do something—before they tore someone else apart.

But do what? *With* what?

"We can do everything, get ready for everything, right here on our own ground." His father's words came back to him. But the .22 was only a single-shot practice gun that Dad had used to teach Mom and him to shoot. It wasn't much good on anything bigger than a squirrel. The sixteen-gauge could hit hard, but it kicked hard too. It would be easy to miss, and it carried only two shells. There were at least three dogs. He'd heard there were five. Dad should have them better prepared!

But there was no making anything any different now. Cliff went back to the kitchen door and stood looking out at the pasture, which was like a green rug shoved up against the walls of trees. It'd been cleared a long time before. The stumps were all gone and the trunks probably hauled off to be milled. Only bits of charcoal in the earth, if you knew where to look, told where the leftover limbs had been burned. The pasture's edges were fuzzy because of the brush creeping back to reclaim the land. "Those sheep," Dad was sure, "they'll hold back that brush."

The sheep were resting peacefully right beside the brush as Cliff tried to slow down his excitement and think more calmly. He hated to drive the sheep in now and make them lose their evening graze. He hated the idea of anyone missing out on doing something he wanted to.

He wished he had an older brother like Len, someone who could help with chores and then drive in to practice afterward. But there was still no changing anything. He'd probably have gotten a brother just like Eddie. He was just as well off being alone.

"On our own ground we can do things on our own."

Okay.

Cliff returned inside to load the shotgun and fix himself a quick snack, in between darting back and forth to the door to watch the sheep. He knew what he was going to do.

4 «

As they'd raced away from the squealing school bus, the two tall brown dogs had leaped into the lead. They raced each other into the woods and out of sight of the road. The big gray dog had been several springing jumps behind as he'd followed the creek into the shallow gulley in the woods. Then all alone he'd swerved and scrambled up one of the banks. He'd reached the lip of a ridge, and there he crawled into a leafy thicket and let his legs stop. He lay, hiding, watching his back trail, panting with his tongue way out and fringed with thin bubbly slobber. His sides shook as he panted rapidly. If nothing was following him he would rest. If danger was coming closer he'd spy it in time to move again. If that danger was an animal, even a man now, he might hungrily attack from ambush.

The two brown dogs were still straining for speed in the soft, muddy bottom of the gulley, and dodging all the washed-bare roots that stuck out from both sides. They'd been raised together on an estate near Duluth by a man who was afraid his money might make him a target for kidnappers. If he had known of the gray dog, he might have welcomed him. From the time they were half grown the two brown dogs had pleased him by bounding to investigate—and nearly frighten off—every visitor who'd appeared.

On almost any day they both could have simply trotted out the open gateway of the estate and left, but they'd never thought of it. They'd had each other's company and plenty of running room, and they'd always found enough food and attention to keep them around the house.

Then, one moonless night a year and a half ago, the bouncing white flicker of a startled rabbit's tail had caught their fancy and they'd chased it. The rabbit had scooted through a small hole in the estate's fence. Strong and eager, the two dogs had leaped over the top. They had been able to find neither the rabbit nor an easy way back in, for the gates were closed at night, and they'd begun to roam about. Exploring new places was exciting, and they'd kept at it.

After three days of loping and poking around haphazardly they'd discovered many things, but no food. Hunger had been forcing them home when they'd come upon a fisherman wading along the edge of a rapids in the St. Louis River. They'd caught a strong scent of fresh trout from the man's creel, and they'd startled him by bounding closer to investigate.

With a gasp he'd stepped backward. In his hurry he'd forgotten the push of the water over the slippery rocks. He'd tried to move as if he were still on dry land, and he had fallen. The close scent of food from the creel, then the man's obvious weakness, had stirred the dogs even more. They'd jumped closer.

"Get away from me! Get away!" The man cursed and shouted. The force of the water kept him staggering to one side as he tried to stand up again. The busy rush of the water all about made the dogs more excited too, but the anger in the man's voice was frightening and made them hesitate.

Up on one knee, the man threatened them with his pole. "Back off! Get away!"

Unsure, tensed between hunger and fear, ready to chase if he ran, the dogs didn't move.

He struck at them. The narrow tip of the fishing rod whipped against one of them. It did no harm, but it stung. Feeling attacked, in a rage of self-defense, the stung dog fought back. The other dog jumped with him. Before the man could start to scream he was down and the water was gagging him. The creel with its fish went underneath him. The dogs couldn't find it and began snapping at his kicking legs. They ripped his pants, then bit at the warm flesh they found beneath. They tore at him only briefly, for the unusual thing they were doing made them nervous and restless. But the man had fainted. They left him with his head underwater and a gashed artery in his leg. He was soon dead.

The current gradually loosened his body and carried it for half a mile. That night a foraging bear found him. The next day searchers found bear tracks beside the man's bones. They hunted the bear and shot her. What they found in her stomach proved to their satisfaction that she'd been the killer.

Meanwhile the two brown dogs, in their new excitement, had run deeper into the woods. They'd discovered deer and the thrill of the chase. They'd begun to spend their time just looking for deer to chase, but they hadn't done it very cleverly, and had caught none until the deep snows came to help them. All autumn, before the snow, they'd had to eat by pouncing on mice and slow grouse that were too fat and busy getting ready for winter to get away. Like most carnivores the dogs could run a long way on little food if they had to.

Now they were wearing themselves out, trying to outrace this newest excitement by galloping along the soft gulley. It led them to a bog and they plunged on through it the same way they'd crossed the bog by the clearing. This time they suddenly reached the edge of open water. Two Moon Lake. In panic they floundered about in a bottomless ooze before they could get turned around.

Slow and bedraggled, they plodded back up the shallow gulley. They scented the place where the large gray dog had climbed out, hauled themselves up the bank, and collapsed exhaustedly beside him.

The gray dog could smell where they'd been, but he didn't know what had seen them and might be following. He lay very still and alert. Suddenly he saw fluttering movements out over the field next to the road. He watched as a flock of traveling crows settled down there.

He stared as the crows began to scratch and peck for the newly planted seeds, and decided there was no way he could hope to catch one. Aching from hunger, he pushed up onto his feet and moved away at a trot. The tall brown dogs were in a mood to be led, so weary or not, they followed.

The gray dog trotted along the ridgetop, which soon divided into two separate ridges. The forest-land between the lakes and bogs was a maze of such ridges, and the fork that the gray dog took divided again and again. He never hesitated; he always seemed to know which choice to make.

He slowed into a crouching walk. The brown dogs crouched forward too, and they all squirmed under a fence of old slack barbed wire and on into a wide raspberry thicket. They were out of the forest. Above them the northern sun was still high; between the leaves of the berry bushes there was bright blue sky. As they crept through the thicket the scent of other animals came strongly: the scents of body heat, chewed grass, droppings, and an oily smell of sweat beneath wool.

The mood of the two brown dogs changed immediately from weariness back to hunger. They followed the movements of the gray dog, who began to advance in a catlike way—step-pause, step-pause—very slowly among the bushes. His eyes were glaring, his jaws parted a little in anticipation, as he got to where he could see the sheep. They were lying down. The nearest was only several jumps away.

The brown dogs inched up beside him. The gray dog made several short sharp movements with his tail against the ground, and he met their staring attention with glaring eyes of his own. His meaning was clear, and the two brown dogs hesitated, then stayed behind him.

He looked again toward the sheep. He had always found these animals shut behind tall boards at night. Now they were exposed—and he was even more wary of open daylight. So again, despite his hunger, he would stay waiting a bit—watching, listening, scenting.

Out in front of him some of the sheep began to stir. A movement far across the pasture was drawing their attention. An upright figure had come out of the woods there, trotting steadily, carrying a gun.

As the man came closer, some of the sheep stood up, then a few burst into a run. The other sheep caught the alarm. They jumped up and ran too, most not knowing where to go or why. Those sheep that were closer to the man and had seen him ran from him toward the bushes. Those that were farther away hadn't seen him and ran away from the shadowy bushes. The whole flock came together, milled in a circle, and abruptly stopped, waiting for some other hint. There was none. The man had stopped. The sheep all looked toward him; he was the only thing different they could see. The dogs in the thicket were motionless. The air was still.

After a few moments the man decided the sheep had calmed down. He began trotting steadily again, past the sheep, in the same direction he'd been heading.

There were no sheep near the raspberries now. They all stood together in the middle of the slope, eyes toward the trotting man.

The gray dog crept forward to the edge of the thicket. The two brown dogs immediately moved forward beside him. Now they could see the buildings and corrals at the lower edge of the pasture and the man growing smaller as he ran in that direction. Quickly the gray dog shifted his crouch, his tail swung into a different curve, he twitched his ears to a higher angle. Somewhere in those movements he signaled to the brown dogs what he planned to do.

5 «

While the gray dog was leading the two others under the slack-wire fence in the woods, Cliff was two steps to the side of third base—in front of the tool-shed and the corrals.

"Little by little you can learn the main things, how to throw and swing, alone," Dad had said many times. And Cliff wanted to believe it. He had to believe it.

He spread his legs just a certain amount, bent his

knees slightly, and then set his right foot back a little. He held his glove low. All his practicing had made him feel that it was from this position that he could most quickly spring forward or to the sides.

He glanced over his shoulder as a third baseman would, to keep check on the flag in center field, to be sure which way the wind would blow a high pop fly. What he saw was the sheep still lying calmly high up in the pasture.

Then he stared forward at his stone-and-cement batter.

Two years ago Dad had driven him in the pickup almost all the way to Duluth to lug those hefty rocks from the bed of the St. Louis River. In the country where their farm was there were light sandy soils and heavy gumbo soils, but big rocks were as scarce as whales. The short wall they'd built was as tall as Cliff. It could take a lot of beating and deflect a thrown ball every way a bat might. It stood as a kind of monument, reminding him how sure Dad was that he could learn to play ball all by himself.

The rocks could also tear up leather, so the balls he used were hard-rubber, wet-weather baseballs. He'd discovered that they bounced off better than thrown rocks would have, but not a whole lot better, so he had to stand very close. He decided to try pretending an outside pitch to a right-handed batter.

For an instant he had to straighten a little as he flung the ball hard at a certain bulge of the knobby wall. Yet in the same motion he sprang to his left as a third baseman would, toward where an outside pitch would most likely be hit.

The ball came back low near his trailing foot. He braked with his spikes and shoved his body around, and backhanded the ball on its short hop. Then he couldn't raise up quickly enough to throw directly to first base, so he completed his spin, took a stride, and then threw as hard as he could at the burlap sack hung in a pile of old hay bales. The ball sailed across a hundred feet of farmyard and sank into a corner of its target.

"Hey, now!" he exclaimed, and stood celebrating the bull's-eye with himself. Then he picked another ball off the ground near him.

"But too much arc," he had to admit out loud. "Got to get those throws more level."

He pitched at the rocks again, and the ball banged right back at him, throat high. He grabbed it and threw, trying to make the ball go straighter and faster than before, and felt right away that he'd missed. He watched the ball strike the ground in front of the hay and skitter off.

"Too low." He shook his head. He began thoughtfully stepping about, testing various ways of coordinating his stride with the movement of his arm. He wished he could practice on more than thirty grounders a day, but hard-rubber balls were heavy, and Dad had warned him it would strain his throwing arm to do more. He needed someone to hit to him. He'd even tried to think of ways that Bandanna might help him, but the dog had all the wrong equipment and all the wrong ideas.

Bandanna had gradually learned that his participation in these games was no longer welcome. He lay, head on paws, out of the way. His ears wrinkled forward and his eyes opened wider every time Cliff spoke, then his hairy face relaxed and looked sleepy as Cliff became silent again.

Cliff picked the last ball of his six-ball set from the ground. He had two balls with holes drilled in them hanging on stiff wires, one under a tree by the house, the other in the barn where he worked out in rainy or wintry weather. He'd worked up to taking a hundred cuts a day at them with his bat, strengthening his shoulders, sharpening his eyes.

"You can do that even when no one else can *have* any practice," Dad had always reminded him.

But today was good baseball weather. At the park in town they'd be practicing, then choosing up for a game.

Silently Cliff got himself set again, two steps off

his third base. He glanced over his shoulder toward the imaginary flagpole—

The sheep were running! They were running away from the hilltop woods and some were running up toward the woods. They were being run in a circle! He could think of only one reason.

He dropped the ball and shook loose his glove. He started for the shotgun he'd leaned against the shed with a handful of extra shells. Then he changed his mind and went to grab Bandanna to put him in the shed so he wouldn't go charging out there. He'd be no match for a wild dog pack, and he'd be in the way of any shooting.

He lunged toward Bandanna, and Bandanna started to rise, not knowing if they were going to romp together, or if he'd done something wrong. But Cliff stopped again, deciding he ought to get quickly back to the phone. He could get the dog into the house before he smelled or saw anything in the pasture.

"C'mon, Banda! C'mon, boy!" He spoke sharply and slapped at his leg urgently as he started toward the house, then he pivoted back to get the gun. He grabbed it with one hand, scooping the extra shells up into his pocket with the other, then stopped short. The shotgun couldn't shoot far into the pasture but the sound might scare off the dog pack. It'd only take a moment; it might save a sheep.

"Get down! Sit!" he ordered Bandanna, hoping his voice would keep the dog behind the shed and board corrals, away from any contact with the pasture for just a moment longer. At the same time Cliff quickly looked around the corner of the shed. He raised the shotgun to point out over the tops of the corrals toward the slope. The sheep had stopped running, and he saw it was not wild dogs that had disturbed them, but a person trotting closer across the grass.

As he lowered the gun he recognized who it was. With a scowl of annoyance he set the shotgun back down. His heart was thumping, his breath coming heavily, there was a leftover chill tingling down his spine. He moved to get his glove and ball, still trying to shake off the fluster that the false alarm had brought on.

At the same time Bandanna, all roused up with nowhere to go, went bounding about on his own. He careered out beyond the corral boards and discovered there was something different off in the pasture. Bandanna gave out a low growl. The loose black-and-white fur on his neck rose and he went forward on stiff, tense legs.

The visitor shouted once, then again, and Bandanna's hackles lay down, his legs relaxed, his tail began a slow expectant wagging. The voice of Eddie Massek was familiar enough to be remembered. Ban-

danna stepped between the ancient wires of the pasture fence, then ran forward to sniff Eddie Massek and seek a greeting.

Eddie reached the old fence. He set his carbine through, then grabbed a fence post and vaulted over, picked up the gun, and came bouncing closer. His round, puffy face that was always popping over the seat back in the school bus to tease Cliff about his daydreaming was red from running.

Eddie came closer, with Bandanna at his heels and the carbine held point upwards in his hands. "Hey!" he cried out. "What're you doing?"

Cliff had regathered his rubber baseballs, and five of them lay on the ground behind him. He held the other in his hand, ready to throw at the rock wall. Most of his panic at seeing the sheep run had drained out of him. "Practicing!" he answered strongly.

"Baseball!" Eddie exclaimed. He came to a halt and spoke as fast as he could between deep breaths. "What good's . . . that going to do . . . with those . . . wild dogs we saw . . . loose out there!"

"I made the phone calls. And those sheep haven't even started their afternoon graze yet." Cliff fingered the ball and looked directly back at Eddie. "I saw it was you spooking them."

"You're wasting time!" Eddie practically shouted at him. "You oughtta be out looking for those dogs!"

"I can see the pasture from here," Cliff told him. He purposefully turned his attention toward the rock wall again, hoping that for once Eddie would believe he was serious. "I've got no one to call me to practice. I've got to keep my own schedule."

"Stupid baseball! It's where those dogs are that counts!" Eddie yelled at him.

Cliff slowly shook his head. "*I* can't do anything about those dogs. I already thought about it." He shifted his legs into position and stretched into a careful throwing windup. "There's a bat in the shed. Why don't you see if you can hit?"

Eddie stepped in front of him. "They've got to be up in those woods. Maybe so close that they saw me out in your pasture too. We ought to go after them."

Cliff dropped his arms impatiently. Eddie was forever full of projects: duck blinds to build, a snowmobile to overhaul; even regular farm chores like fixing fence and spring-cleaning the barn excited him. But not sports. At school he'd laugh and say, "You baseballers look just like pups chasing after a big white rabbit's tail."

"You talk about chasing rabbit tails!" Cliff said, his temper rising. "Those dogs could be anywhere. There's no point in trying to find them alone. Not just the two of us against five, guns or no guns. Not in those thick woods."

"There's only three of them," Eddie answered.

"We only *saw* three, but Karla's dad said there were five jumping for her when he saved her."

"They shot two this afternoon."

"Who said?"

"Ma, when I got home. They baited them near Felters'. Someone called Ma and said they got two and had the rest cornered in a slough. Pa went with the posse to squeeze the trap."

Cliff looked harder at Eddie. "But they *don't* have them trapped. We saw them from the bus. At least Karla sure thought it was them."

"That's what I told Ma. She drove over to tell Pa and the others to come this way, so I ducked Sis and grabbed the carbine and came over here."

"But those dogs could double back. They could be anywhere," Cliff reasoned.

"No." Eddie shook his head so hard his hair flopped. He seemed to be grinning even when his lips turned down seriously. He said, "They won't cut back right now, knowing they're being hunted and after Phil stopped the bus like he did. I don't figure they'll swim Two Moon Lake either. They've got to be up in your woods."

Cliff was still looking hard at Eddie, thinking closely about what he was saying. Two Moon Lake was mostly to the east, but a thumb-shaped bay swung around to the north as well. If the dogs kept on the move they'd have to get around Winter Bay. They'd *have* to pass somewhere through the woods above the sheep pasture.

"I'd better get our sheep in *now*," Cliff decided. He let the ball drop with the others, shook off his glove, and started once more for the shotgun. "If those hounds are that close!"

"Right!" Eddie nodded vigorously and bounced along beside him. "Then we've got to run to Stony Creek."

"What for?" Cliff picked up the shotgun and started for the pasture.

"Because if they don't stop to hunt, they'll cross that creek soon," Eddie said. "And if they get across it they'll be into woods where *no* one'll find them. Not till they kill something again."

Cliff paused and breathed deeply. There was one big gaping hole in Eddie's logic. "I'm not going over there with just the two of us," Cliff snapped. "That's crazy."

"It's not crazy!" Eddie was directly in front of him again, practically jumping up and down. "If we get there first we might get a shot. At least scare 'em back."

"There aren't even any trees to climb over there,"

Cliff argued. "And the brush is so thick you can't see." He wanted to go on and get the sheep in, but Eddie stayed in front of him.

For once the twist of Eddie's mouth was bitter. "We gotta go there," he shouted angrily. "We gotta try to keep them back till Pa and the rest of them catch up!"

Cliff was angry too. "I'll wait and go with them. I don't need any leg torn up and shortened like Karla's. Not yet!"

He started to step around Eddie, but Eddie grabbed his arm. "We gotta—"

Cliff jerked his arm away. "I'm just going—"

Bandanna cut them off with a deep, harsh growl. His hackles were raised as he moved past them, stiff legged and not too fast, head outstretched. He looked uncertain, but he'd sensed some alarm.

Cliff was immediately alert again to things besides Eddie. He heard a rattling, like sprayed gravel or hail, a drumming sound beating harder and closer. He shoved past Eddie and sprang to the corner of the shed. The sheep were running again, but this time they were moving headlong down toward the corrals. The ground was still too damp with spring for them to raise much dust, and Cliff could see clearly behind them. Two sheep were lying in the pasture and three large dogs—a gray one and two dark ones like the three he'd seen from the bus—were snapping at them.

Bandanna was off by the fence line, jumping from side to side, his attention all on the charging flock.

"Banda! Here! Here!" Cliff shouted. He set aside the shotgun and ran to get his dog before Bandanna got wind of the wild dogs. All stirred up, Bandanna came running to Cliff's voice, then tried to scoot away. Cliff grabbed him with both hands. Behind him he heard Eddie's carbine explode, and explode again, and once more.

6 «

There had been other times and other places when the gray dog had lay hidden and secretly watched men come near him with guns and then go away, as the trotting man had done. Right after such times he'd always been able to move about safely. So while Cliff and Eddie were arguing the gray dog had hurriedly threaded his way among the thick raspberry bushes. When he'd reached the edge of the pasture, he'd leaped forward to attack, his hunger pushing him on as fiercely as a wave of anger. The two brown dogs had sprung close behind him.

In swift low bounds they'd moved between the sheep and the corrals, and the whole flock had stampeded uphill, away from the corrals. But the sheep had been able to see no opening in the thick berry bushes, and they'd swerved around and stopped, already hot and panting under their winter-heavy wool.

The gray dog charged straight at them. Several sheep came stomping forward, heads tucked low for butting. All three dogs dodged aside, surprised to be met by an attack.

Immediately the whole flock broke through the openings between the dogs and went running down the slope toward the corrals, their small hoofs creating a low thunder.

The gray dog let the main rush go by. Then he bounded at the rear of the flock where the slower sheep were being left behind. He and the two brown dogs chased a small bunch aside. The three of them snarled and leaped and snapped, trying to drive that bunch into the shelter of the woods.

The separated sheep bolted in a group this way and that, more frightened of being separated from the flock than they were of the dogs. They dashed again toward the corrals. Several of them tried to butt past, but the gray dog was ready for that and jumped at the nearest ewe, knocking her nearly breathless on her side. He gagged on two mouthfuls of wool before his teeth finally broke through the warm soft skin of the throat and cut the jugular vein, while the ewe kicked weakly at his shoulder.

The two brown dogs had dragged down another sheep. All three were so excited by their kills and tore so eagerly at their food that they didn't hear either the explosion from far below the slope or the faint quick buzz of the bullet zipping past. They didn't notice the next explosion, or the third either, but they did hear a loud *shunk* as the brown dog with the darker-colored ears scrambled sideways with a shrill yelp and fell over. The two others jerked their heads up and stared at him. They all heard the next explosion, and the wallop of something hitting the ground beneath the gray dog's chest.

The gray dog abandoned his food and raced for the woods, and the pale-eared brown dog went springing past him. The wounded brown dog staggered to his feet. He heard another explosion as something burned across the top of his hip. He started to run. Pain shocked him with every step, forcing him to twitch and jump. He was awkward, but still light and speedy, and he was soon in the woods trying to find the way the others had gone by their scent.

The gray dog hadn't slowed down. As soon as he'd reached the shelter of the woods he'd become calmer, but he'd kept running as hard as he could, circling back to the edge of the pasture higher along the hill where there were no berries. It was his method when disturbed to first double back and spy on things behind him.

But this panicked dash had sapped his energy. Lately he'd been having to dodge more and more men in the woods, and those few quick nips of food were all he'd been able to get for several days. His muscles ached as sharply as his stomach and tightened up as he tried to relax. He lay down a different way, then found himself forced to shift again from one hurting position into another.

His senses began to fight each other. He had learned his way around this area, and he knew that if danger pressed him closer his only escape could be north, through a small brushy valley, across a creek, and into a bigger woods that he didn't know much about. He felt he ought to be going there. That was the kind of retreat he'd always made.

But now hunger held him. Close behind was food he would not have to find or chase or kill. Perhaps the danger would go away.

Meanwhile the brown dog with the pale ears had leaped along other ridges till he'd come to the edge of Two Moon Lake again. He paused and scented around uncertainly and discovered he'd been running alone. He raced back the way he'd come, and met his injured brother hobbling toward him.

The injured dog sank down into a bed of old leaves that filled a hollow where a tree had once fallen and rotted away. He lay in the cool, damp softness, panting and twitching. The pale-eared dog stood breathing heavily beside him for a while, unable to plan what to do next. Then he took a notion and the urge pushed aside his weariness. He quickly signaled the wounded dog, then trotted farther back through the woods. At the end of the raspberries he stopped.

He saw there were two men in the pasture. Both were standing right beside the food he'd left behind. His urgent hunger goaded him to attack, but by himself he could not quite gather enough boldness, not yet. He lay down in the berry thicket, forced to patience and to watching, as his boldness started growing.

7 «

As Eddie shot, and shot again, Bandanna tried to squirm free. Cliff held him by the hind legs and dragged him toward the shed like a wriggling wheelbarrow. The carbine roared for the fourth time. He swung Bandanna into the shed and slammed the door just as the carbine exploded again.

"Did you hit any?" he shouted. He ran from the shed door to look. The sheep were crowding and leaping to get in through the corral's open gateway.

Up on the hill he saw one of the dark dogs hop crookedly into the raspberry thickets.

"I had one down!" Eddie yelled back. He was running toward the pasture fence. "Now he's getting away!"

"Where're the others?"

"Up in those woods!" Eddie yelled.

"Wait!" Cliff shouted. "We gotta shut—"

Eddie wasn't waiting. He paused to slide the carbine out in front of him, then quickly crawled through the fence.

Cliff grabbed a corral post beside him and vaulted over and in among the sheep. They were cramming together into one corner of the corral. Bandanna was barking and whining excitedly inside the shed. Cliff struggled as fast as he could to get his legs between the sheep and over their backs and over to where he could close the corral gate.

From there he could still hear Bandanna's barking adding to his own excitement. He saw Eddie running across the pasture toward the fallen ewes, and he started to follow but once more remembered the shotgun. He fumed at himself for being so half-cocked under pressure as he clambered back over the gate he'd just closed, dashed around the sheep in the corrals, and vaulted back out. He got the shotgun from beside the shed, ran along the corrals to the old

wire fence, slid the shotgun under, and crawled through the way Eddie had done. Already breathing hard, he pumped his legs uphill. Eddie was already almost beside the nearest ewe that was down.

Both ewes were torn and bloody. Their eyes were glazed. A few early-season flies were quickly settling on them.

Cliff had seen dead sheep before. He'd seen them die suddenly or slowly, killed neatly by diseases with fancy names like enterotoxemia or tetanus that left no gaping wounds. He'd seen the blood spurt from the nostrils of other sheep when Dad had shot them in the corrals, and he had helped to hang and skin them, and later to cut them up for the freezer.

None of that dying had ever been pleasant. But you expected sicknesses sooner or later, and you planned for them. At slaughter time you thought of good food later on, or that the same thing would happen if you sent them to market, or that you had to kill something to eat.

He stood staring down at the ewe that the gray dog had killed. His thoughts grew hot and vibrated in his head stronger than any anger he'd ever felt before. This was an attack on him too. And on Mom and Dad. It wasn't just a hundred dollars lying wasted that they couldn't easily afford. It was two friends found murdered after a raid. *Kill them!* his thoughts hammered. *Find those dogs and kill them!*

"C'mon! Across the pasture!" Eddie shouted at him. "They'll run into the woods. Maybe they'll slow up. Maybe we can beat them to Stony Creek!"

"Wait!" Cliff shouted at him again. "No one'll know where we're looking."

Eddie barely hesitated. "They'll find Bandanna locked in, and the corrals shut. They'll see these dead sheep."

"But—" Cliff started.

"All right!" Eddie exclaimed. "We'll leave a message. Here." He set his weight on one foot and began cutting rapidly at the soft ground with the heel of his other boot. "I'll dig the shaft. You do the points."

Cliff understood, and together they chopped their heels at the turf, quickly cutting an arrow that pointed toward the pasture's far northwest corner.

Then they went jogging in that direction as fast as they could.

8 «

The gray dog crouched in the damp shadows at the edge of the woods, and watched the two men with guns go trotting by a little in front of him. He made no movement, though his nerves stirred with the warning that now there were men crowding him on all sides.

He saw the two men climb over a high fence, then go out of sight onto the woods at the far corner of the pasture. They were moving in the direction of the big woods, where the gray dog had planned to escape. He felt an urge to run, to get there first, and another urge to wait until dark and the chance to eat. He stretched his muscles restlessly. The war of urges in his head became fiercer. He shifted with nervous fear and uttered a hungry whine.

A year ago, after he'd survived his first winter in the area around him, his experience and his remaining strength had been equal to that of the two brown dogs combined. So instead of fighting when they'd met, they'd begun hunting together. It had been the first companionship he'd ever had. Later the two smaller dogs had joined them, and he'd found that five dogs could warm a hollow in the snow much better than one could. Five dogs could run deer easier than one. He was not anxious to leave such good country.

But spring was the roughest season. Food had become steadily scarcer through the winter. The thawing ground was moist and chill almost everywhere he tried to rest. He'd been forced to forage with the others in the daytime. Once they'd scented loose chickens, and had fought off the young girl who'd discovered them—but then they'd been attacked and forced to run by a yelling man arriving fast on a huge, growling tractor.

Twice today, as they'd tried to hunt in daylight,

danger had struck at the dogs he was with.

A movement at the corner of his vision made him focus both eyes down the pasture. Immediately a low angry growl stirred in his throat. One of the brown dogs had bounded back into the pasture, making for the food that lay there.

His growl became a steady, threatening rumble, warning the brown dog to leave the food alone till he was ready. The brown dog was too far away to hear him. The gray dog crouched forward tensely. More opposite urges—to wait, to rush down for the food—fought on inside him.

He hesitated. It was daylight, and there were men nearby. Gradually his anger subsided. He would return to his old habits. He would hunt and eat alone. He would wait until dark for his food.

While he had waited, several armed men from the posse had reached the shallow gulley where he'd run to escape the school bus and were trying to decide where the dogs had gone next. The crows had flapped away in fright from the seeded field when the men had arrived there, and had flown fast for a couple miles. They were quietly settling to rest in the treetops of the woods behind the gray dog. But he could see only the brown dog out in the pasture, greedily tearing away at the food.

Other things caught his attention. His ears stiffened,

picking up the faint chugging sounds of motors, then the dim excited barking of a dog. He knew what the sounds were, though he couldn't tell yet what they meant. They did not sound unusual coming from the distant farmyard.

Down in the farmyard six other men from the posse were hurrying away from a pickup and a Jeep to see if anyone was home. They heard a dog barking in a shed. They saw a glove and some baseballs scattered on the ground. Before they had a chance to notice the sheep in the closed corral, one of them saw the brown dog and dead sheep up in the pasture and shouted, "There!"

Three men leaped back to brace their guns against fenders and hoods. Two simply sank down on their knees to steady their aim. The man who'd yelled ran to use the firm corner of the shed. Before he got there the shooting had started.

The gray dog had heard the thin rattle of a voice. Then harsh, thumping roars broke out from down near the corrals and came snarling up past him like strong gusts of wind, echoing and reechoing stormily in the trees all around the pasture. As the first echoes passed, he heard also the startled cawing of crows from somewhere.

He looked quickly around, trying to understand such commotions from every direction. As the echoes faded, he saw the brown dog lying still beside the sheep, and immediately he understood.

In the woods the injured brown dog had squirmed deeper into the leaves. He understood where his brother had gone and that at some time he'd be back with a mouthful of food to drop in front of him. He lay still, trying to fight his pain. His mind was cutting it off by fuzzing into a slight stupor. He heard the roars, but it was the raucous swarm of crows above him that woke him most. He came awake with a thirst much sharper than his hunger. He could scent the lake nearby, and he struggled to get up. His torn muscles had begun to draw together tightly; he could barely get to his feet, and a swaying stagger was the smoothest movement he could make. His jerkiness started his wounds bleeding again. He grew weaker and had to sink back to the ground. Slowly his eyes began to glaze.

The men in the farmyard had jumped back into their vehicles and headed for the pasture gate. They drove up to where the dog they'd shot lay dead. The pickup came to a stop over the dug arrow point, hiding it from view. The driver took a microphone off a hook on the dashboard and spoke briefly by radio to others in the posse. Two men threw the dead dog into the back of the pickup. Another found a splotchy blood trail. Then as fast as they could the six men began moving ahead on foot, following the blood trail through the raspberry thicket.

Swiftly and smoothly, the gray dog had swung away from the pasture edge right after the shooting. He moved along a ridge in a low, hurried, but cautious crouch, for he knew there were two men ahead of him. He had no doubt about being in a closing trap now. He could not wait till dark. He would have to get across the small creek valley and make his way into the unfamiliar woods of the new country beyond.

9 «

While the gray dog had silently and secretly watched them from the woods, Cliff had jogged with Eddie all the way up to the northwest corner of the pasture. There they'd reached the new woven-wire fencing, taller than their heads. By last fall Dad had saved up enough to buy the wire, and Cliff had helped stretch it to the posts he'd already helped cut and set.

"Just got to keep after it, little by little on our own," Dad had said. "We'll have our whole pasture as bearproof and dogproof as you can get."

The new fence had been hard to climb over, especially since they'd had to be careful with the guns, yet not set them out of reach either. Once over, they hadn't stopped to catch their breath but hurriedly made their way into the woods. They were soon surrounded by shadowy hiding places, and Cliff strongly suspected they shouldn't have come. He felt twice in his pocket to be sure the extra shells he'd scooped up were still there. He wondered how long it would take him to reload in a hurry.

A short distance into the woods the ground dipped suddenly down into the creek valley. There were no trees that anyone could climb on that slope, just lots of the tall woody brush he remembered, thick with leaves that blocked the sunshine and kept the steep ground slippery with damp mud.

"A whole pack of dogs could be in this stuff," Cliff whispered as they started down, "and we'd never see them."

"But they could smell us." Eddie whispered too. "That could spook them right back to where my pa and those other men should be coming."

"Unless it spooks them into attacking us." Cliff's muscles were tense all through him.

Eddie's round freckled face looked back at him, his eyes seeming to sparkle with excitement. "Let them try it! There's only three, and one of them's wounded. We could get them by ourselves!"

"We couldn't see them in time—" Cliff started to insist, but Eddie flung his arms out wildly.

Cliff jolted in fright and swept his shotgun about, trying to be ready in all directions at once. Then he realized that Eddie's feet had simply slipped beneath him, and that Eddie had only been grabbing at brush to keep from flopping on his back.

That alarm over, they eased farther down the hill. Cliff wasn't having as much trouble staying upright as he'd expected, not nearly as much as Eddie. He realized he still had on his baseball spikes.

"We'll be able to see pretty quick," Eddie hissed. And after Eddie made a few more awkward skids, they came onto almost level footing, out into a narrow slot of open air where the creek flowed.

Stony Creek was the lower part of a slough that carried water from Cabin Lake to Two Moon Lake. As the slough funneled between two close forest ridges, its water was squeezed and forced to flow faster. The faster water had cut a straight channel down to a bed of fist-sized stones that had been left behind and buried after ancient glaciers had dug the lakes and pushed up the ridges. The stones were worn as smooth as eggs beneath the sun-sparkled water, but the edge of the creek was sticky with mud, and Eddie immediately began studying the mud for footprints.

Cliff looked nervously back at the tall brush they'd just come through. That brush was still only a strong leap away from them.

The slope across the creek was just as steep and brushy, except toward Two Moon Lake there were bare places where some of the soft dirt had slipped downward of its own weight. Cliff quickly scanned the brush on both sides beyond the slide area—downstream, till he was looking straight out the opening where the creek reached the broad water of Winter Bay. Then upstream, till his eyes met the cattails at the edge of the bog where the creek began.

"We'll go up to the bog first," Eddie ordered, "then come back toward the lake. If we don't see any tracks where dogs have crossed, we'll know we've got them trapped."

"*Who*'s trapped?" Cliff responded. "In this bag of brush they've got *us* trapped." When he talked he couldn't listen well for dog sounds, so his voice was pinched and sounded strange even to himself. He wished he hadn't let himself get so blind mad about those two ewes.

"What're you scared of?" Eddie didn't turn his head. His voice, over his shoulder, was quiet but had a cheerful, carefree ring to it.

Cliff felt he was being teased. "What do you think I'm scared of?" he snapped. "Getting torn apart, that's what. They could be on us in a second." Those reasons seemed as clear and big as boulders to Cliff; only a dunce would laugh at them.

Eddie spun around to face him. He was tense, full of enthusiasm that Cliff was dragging down. "How're you going to help if you're scared?" he scolded sharply. "We've got guns. You've got two quick barrels. You can pull those triggers quicker'n I can crank this carbine. Quicker'n anything can jump."

"But I've still got to hit. Suppose there's no time to aim?"

"If they're close you won't have to aim!" Eddie's voice got sharper, more impatient. "You going to help or not? You're scared you'll have to aim, but you're scared they'll be too close. How're you ever going to play baseball, scared of anyone who comes sliding in?"

Cliff had faced that question before. Automatically he gave the same hopeful answer he'd given himself while practicing at home alone. "There'd be only one guy, and I'd see him coming."

But Eddie hadn't waited for an answer. He'd spun away and focused his attention back on the mud along the creek. "C'mon," he ordered. "Let's keep moving. You keep your eyes on that brush. If I find any tracks, we're too late. You can go back to playing games. You can let those dogs go off and kill something else."

You think *this* is a game, Cliff thought angrily, but he kept it to himself. Arguing was too noisy. He followed Eddie along the creek, listening and watching even while he paused to shake off mud that clung to his spikes.

It wasn't like knocking mud off your spikes in a batter's box and getting ready to see how well you could hit. It wasn't like watching for a catcher's signals to see if you could guess where a batted ball would be hit so you could get to it. This was no fun at all. This was worse than trying to field line drives at third base blindfolded. It's dumb, stupid, being down in here! Cliff fumed. But he was here, and it felt safer to stay than to start back alone through the brush.

The mud softened their footsteps. The little creek was too full to gurgle over the stones. No breeze reached down into its narrow valley. When they didn't talk, there was almost no sound. Cliff began to notice the increasing number of mosquitoes, and when they got to the bog, the mosquitoes rose around them like thin smoke, a humming swarm. He and Eddie had to step hurriedly to the brush and quietly twist off leafy twigs to fan the mosquitoes away. But they found no dog tracks and started back toward the lake. The cloud of mosquitoes followed, making it impossible to be completely alert.

It would've only taken an extra moment, Cliff chafed at himself, to have grabbed up a bottle of insect dope from the—

The flickering of a shadow made both of them flinch and stop and grab their guns with both hands, but it was only a woodpecker looping overhead, coming from somewhere beyond the ridge across the creek toward the woods they'd come through.

"Watch that bird," Eddie hissed. "See if anything up there disturbs it."

Cliff was already watching.

The woodpecker disappeared calmly into the treetops.

"Let's keep moving," Eddie whispered.

But part of Cliff's mind stayed with the free-flying woodpecker. With each step a little bit more of his attention left what he was doing and seemed to soar upward, looking back down restlessly on all that had happened. He saw Karla Dobley again, crying in needless panic, safe inside the bus. He remembered himself running up his driveway, shouting even though he should've remembered that no one was home. He saw the way his fingers had fumbled with the phone, and how he'd jumped back and forth, changing his mind, losing time in front of the shed when he'd first seen the sheep running, and again when he'd seen the wild dogs. Again and again, he'd kept forgetting the shotgun, having to run back for it.

He had finally remembered the shotgun, though, and he had grabbed Bandanna and put him in the shed. But through most of it, he realized, he'd acted in confusion and panic.

"You've got to get real game practice," he heard Len telling him. He could hear Holman barking the same thing, from under that big coach's cap. He'd been dreaming and figuring how he'd fool them, how he'd go into the Legion tryouts and really surprise them. But even just bus-dreaming about being in a real tryout had brought nervous sweat to his hands. He shook his head and shivered at what he might do wrong when he wasn't just throwing at a haystack or swinging at a hanging ball, when lots of people were watching him.

Those worries swarmed at Cliff thicker and sharper than the mosquitoes, blotting out all his alertness to the brushy slope close by him. He stumbled a little in the mud along the creek, and saw himself out on the field at tryouts, missing grounders and throwing badly and swinging stiffly at real pitches because he couldn't decide what to do quickly enough. He saw himself being shoved off every position he tried for, not only

by good players like Len, but even by guys who were just out there horsing around but who would have enough experience to know what they were doing. He'd be cut, and there was no other team around where he could try again.

Now Cliff was angry. He'd been kidding himself, not getting ready at all, always wasting his time doing the wrong thing, being in the wrong place, working at practices that really wouldn't help him.

He stumbled again, harder, and in the extra effort to keep his balance he got even angrier. Dad had encouraged him wrong, told him he could do it on his own, and now he'd gotten so excited he'd let Eddie get him into this narrow gulley where he could so easily be trapped and bitten. A single bite could stiffen a leg or a hand.

He slipped, almost falling into the creek, and realized he wasn't paying attention. "So what?" he growled angrily to himself. "Even if nothing happens here, even if I get to be seventeen or eighteen and can travel around on my own, it won't do me any good because I've got no way to become any better a ballplayer by then than I am now or was last year."

Dad was driving all over three states and into Canada now. He was away almost every week to make enough money to pay for the farm he wanted to build up. Mom drove all over the county selling and delivering housewares door-to-door. That was all right. He still couldn't be angry. Why shouldn't they go after what they wanted? But Len could run out his door and down a few blocks to a ball game. And Eddie could walk out his back door to his hunting and fishing and calf raising. Cliff heated himself into a rage at the injustice. He was the only one he knew who couldn't really go after what he wanted—

He slammed flat into Eddie's back. Somewhere behind him he'd heard the sounds, but he hadn't paid any attention. He hadn't halted suddenly, as Eddie had.

Eddie excitedly told him to stop and listen. Cliff had already stopped, and now he was listening to the last of the echoes, coarsely rolling over him, muffled and dim, then changing to the familiar light cawing of a bunch of distant crows.

"Those were shots," Eddie exclaimed. "From near your place! Those dogs must've gone back for the sheep."

"They must've shot them all." Cliff reacted with hope. But his voice was full of the rage his thoughts had been holding.

"Or missed as the dogs ran off," Eddie countered

with hopeful excitement. "Listen to those crows! They're off to that side. I'll bet there's dogs coming our way, and fast."

Cliff thought Eddie might be right, but he couldn't concentrate. He couldn't figure out which way to move, and he had to ask, "What'll we do?"

Eddie knew what to do. He pointed with both hands grasping the carbine. "We've got to be across and up one of those mud slides, so there's no brush in our way. They're going to cross this creek, somewhere in the open. From up there we'll get at least one open shot at them."

Cliff hurriedly looked around. He felt out of place and in the way, and he was still angry about it, but he agreed that up on the slope seemed the safest. "Let's get there!" he said.

They splashed straight down the creek. It was faster than trying to run on the wet mud along the edge. Cliff found that his spikes could catch and cling among the stones as well as Eddie's boots. He didn't worry that the costly shoes were getting soaked.

When they got to the first mud slide they charged it together, jamming the butts of their guns into the ground to pole themselves upward until they reached a protruding root big enough to brace their feet against. There they eased around into a sitting squat.

"I'll watch toward the lake. You watch toward

the bog," Eddie whispered, panting. "Better slap on some mud so we don't have to keep waving at these mosquitoes. Remember, from up here you've got to *aim.*"

Cliff just nodded at every thing Eddie said.

"Those crows!" Eddie suddenly panted. "I'd like to find out how they knew this was going to happen."

Then all Cliff heard was his own breathing and the persistent humming of the mosquitoes. Those were tiny sounds. The new silence in the narrow valley seemed much louder.

10 «

The gray dog was hurrying away from the shooting and the open pasture, but moving carefully in his low crouch, for he remembered there were two men ahead of him. He came onto the ridge where the big trees ended and tall woody brush angled steeply down the hill toward the creek.

This was the way out of the trap that men were trying to draw around him. The smell of clear water was strong. He had not drunk since before beginning to stalk the goat, and a lot of urgent traveling had followed. His thirst tormented him as much as his hunger.

But, as always, he hesitated and cautiously tested the air for a sound or a scent of anything hidden close by. The air was still, and the heavy scent of damp mud and water and crowded trees was all he could find.

Yet he pawed about in indecision. An animal drinking, or just crossing water, was always exposed a little, and not balanced for making quick movements. Freshly drunk water was a bothersome load to have to carry in a hurry, especially in daylight. He had hunted along creeks and shores long enough to know the dangers.

He shied away from the creek and moved on along the wooded ridge until a sharp movement overhead made him freeze. But it was only a small black-and-white bird pecking at the underside of a limb.

He moved farther along the ridge, then stopped as he found the scent of two men who had very recently crossed the ridge. He wanted to dash across the man scent, to stay in the area where he'd learned to hunt, but he knew that straight ahead other pastures opened out, and another big lake would make it hard to move freely. He'd still be in a trap.

His warning senses were pulsing wildly, demanding action. He spun about and ran back along the wooded ridge, under the pecking bird. Simply on blind impulse he chose a place to turn and leap down the hill. He would spring over the creek and dash up into the thick woods beyond.

But the smell of the water came at him very strongly. He dug in his claws to absorb the force, and slowed down near the bottom of the slope. He crept to the creek's edge, stretching out his neck and then his tongue to reach the water.

The cool antimosquito mud had begun to feel heavy on Cliff's skin, as if it might all fall off at any moment. He wondered if this was how a snake felt when shedding its skin. He shifted his head just a little to see if Eddie had done a better job.

Eddie had tightened up his shirt collar, and the dirt that was stuck all over his puffy cheeks made his face look like a gopher mound with two eyes peering out, looking intently at the brushy slope across the creek.

Cliff shifted his glance forward again, and a dry piece of mud fell from his chin and dropped to his sleeve. He twisted his arm just enough to let the mud roll off, and he watched it start a race of other little mudballs down the bare slope. Some of them rolled like three-base hits all the way to the root that braced his feet.

"Man," Eddie murmured tensely beside him.

Cliff jerked his head up alertly. His glance searched the opposite slope. "What is it?" Cliff whispered.

"Just, Man," Eddie breathed. He hadn't seen anything, but he expected to. His body stayed rigid, but his feelings could not be still. "What a way to start the summer!" he whispered. "Outfoxing killer dogs!"

"I'd rather be pouncing on line drives," Cliff muttered.

"Chasing scraps of dead leather." Eddie barely moved his lips, scowling quietly.

"It's fun," Cliff hissed, just loud enough to be heard, which made him feel he had to make his point twice. "More fun than just going from chore to chore."

"Chores get you more'n a bunch of numbers on a board," Eddie mumbled. He tried not to make much sound, but he couldn't let go of the argument either.

"It takes *doing* to put those numbers up there." Cliff's long jaw clenched, and the words squeezed out between his teeth.

"Kids' games," Eddie breathed tightly.

Cliff snorted. "*You* try hitting a curve ball."

"What for?" Eddie gritted his teeth. "I get more fun—"

He stopped. There had been a quick, slight rustling near the top of the woody brush across the creek. Cliff had heard it too. Eddie slowly shifted his carbine to point in that direction. His breath was quick, excited, but confident, as he whispered, "They're coming! Now we'll do something that *counts.*"

Cliff's knees and upper legs and the back of his neck all began to tingle. He felt sweat dampening his palms. He knew that would make the shotgun slippery. This'll count, he echoed silently. And suddenly he felt how badly he still wanted to pounce on grounders and hit at curve balls and work for a score, and a chance to get into pro baseball. He didn't want those teeth tearing into him! His thoughts swung toward panic. He wanted to jump out of this big ditch he was trapped in and run. He had to dig in his heels and press his lips against the earth to hold himself still, telling himself he had to stay on this high open slope so he could use his gun. At what? he thought. Where *are* they?

He saw a movement, a shape, then eyes and a large dog's face. Then the huge gray dog stepped silently out across the mud and tongued at the edge of the creek.

Cliff had to keep himself from pointing too anxiously. He forced his breath to leak out swiftly but softly. "I see one!" Then for a moment, as he breathed back in, he just stared at the dog's face.

"I see," Eddie whispered softly.

"Who shoots?"

"Shh. My carbine, while he's holding still."

From the corner of one eye Cliff saw the carbine move smoothly on one of Eddie's knees, and Eddie's face steadily sinking down behind the sights.

Cliff held his breath. He tried to keep watch for the other dogs, but his eyes kept flicking back to the face he could see, which was still close to the water but was no longer lapping. The big dog was staring about. Cliff could hear his heart thumping. He heard the *snick* as Eddie eased the carbine's hammer back, and the pale dog's eyes seemed to dart their way.

There was a brisk metallic *cleck,* then the quickest instant of silence.

"Ohg!" Eddie seemed to choke. "I forgot to reload."

Cliff saw the huge dog catapult forward, into the air above the creek. He saw the dog land, already disappearing in the nearby brush on the boys' side of the creek. Cliff's panic broke loose. He half stood and jerked up the shotgun, not waiting to aim more than from the hip. His movement shoved the root loose and he slipped, but he shot anyway.

Twice, in quick succession, the shotgun roared and

jumped in his hands as he went sliding down with the loosened mud faster than his eyes could focus. To keep from diving face downward he fell half blindly on his side. He ended in a sudden splash of cold water.

The gray dog's leap had brought him into more brush. He would have sprinted straight uphill through that shelter and into the big woods he was heading for, but suddenly there were two quick roars and the brush ahead of him disintegrated in a shower of splattering mud. His way up the slope to the big woods seemed blocked. In panic he leaped far back from the path of destruction the buckshot had just torn, and landed, without meaning to, in the creek. There he saw two men skidding down. He recognized that they were his danger, and that they were off balance. Despite his panic, or because of it, he fixed on the idea that to be safe he must kill them. He did not hesitate. He charged.

The icy squeeze of the creek water helped send Cliff immediately up onto his feet, into full view of the huge dog coming at him. He saw dark eyes and white teeth in front of a rapidly growing gray shadow.

He still held the emptied shotgun, but there was no

time to swing it hard. He desperately shifted his weight forward toward the charge. Both his wet hands moved to squeeze the shotgun tight by the small part of its stock. He tried to whip it around fast, close against his body, the way he'd learned to choke quick on a bat and punch at a hanging ball if it came swinging close to his chest. This time he couldn't help also tucking down his face and closing his eyes. But he felt the gun barrels strike something solidly. In the same motion the gun flew out of his hands as he was knocked spinning.

He flopped facedown in the water, hoping he'd knocked the dog past him, that he'd have a moment to find the gun again.

He shoved himself up on his hands and knees, and saw the dog springing at Eddie. Eddie's feet were wide apart as he tried to club with the carbine, but he'd cocked his weight back on his heels and couldn't bring the carbine around fast enough. Eddie never completed the swing; he jerked an elbow up in front of his throat and screamed as the dog drove him down, half in water, half on the bank.

Up in the woods between the sheep pasture and Two Moon Lake, the six men had come to a hollow in the ground where a tree had long ago fallen. The dead leaves in the hollow had been stirred up. Many black, rotting ones were now on top, and smears of red blood could be seen clearly on the damp, black humus.

"Look at that blood. It had to stop and rest here," one of the men said, "so it can't be far ahead of us."

"But what about those shots we just heard?"

"I hope that's dog's blood," said another man, "and not from one of those kids."

"It's *got* to be dog's blood!" But that man's voice was shaky and uncertain.

"Where *are* those kids? We should look for them first."

"We gotta look out we don't shoot one of them."

"Or they shoot us."

"Whatever that blood is, we gotta keep—"

A shrill sound, softened by distance, interrupted them, then was gone.

"Was that a man or an animal?"

"That was a scream. Those two shots must've missed!"

"Where'd it come from?"

"Too quick to tell."

"But it was a scream. Someone's in trouble!"

"Those shots were north somewhere. Come on!"

They all followed the man who moved first, breaking their way as fast as they could along a ridge through the woods.

"We're coming!" several of them shouted.

Their yells, loud but blunt, seemed to bounce right back at them from the trees.

Cliff, on his hands and knees when Eddie screamed, had no time to look for the shotgun. He'd have to make sure the barrels were clean and reload anyway before he could shoot. He grasped one of the stones beneath his hands and jumped up, balancing on the slippery footing and throwing hard. For an instant, as his throwing arm streaked forward and down, it was as if he'd hurled himself out of the fight completely. The rough gray fur hunched over Eddie looked like a mound of hay and old burlap. The smooth rock sped straight into the hollowed gut behind the dog's ribs.

With a gnashing howl the gray dog whipped around to slash at the other enemy, but could find nothing there.

Cliff dug up another stone and hurled it with a strength he'd never felt before, but he overthrew. He saw the stone flicker past the dog's ear tips, and then the dog was coming for him again.

He scooped another stone from beneath the sparkle of the water, as fast as he'd ever scooped a ball

bounding off his rock wall. He felt the familiar rhythms as his legs quickly found the balance he'd practiced and his other muscles reacted: It helped him hold off his fear enough to throw again, aiming low. The rock went below the dog's open mouth and struck a leg. Even in his excitement and the dog's splashing he heard the bone break with a crack.

The gray dog stumbled, but lunged on closer. There was no time to scoop again. Cliff leaped sideways and started clawing up the tall mud slope with knees, toes, fingers, spikes.

Unsupported by his broken foreleg, the gray dog couldn't turn as sharply. Yet the big furry body wasn't as bulky or heavy as it looked. Once he got turned and going straight, the gray dog could climb on three legs, and fast.

Cliff had to dodge sideways again, clinging and scuttling crablike across the mud slope. The dog had a harder time turning on the steep, soft footing, and Cliff regained a lead.

Below him he saw Eddie was standing, gaping upward, holding the carbine with one hand but looking dazed. Eddie's other arm hung limply, covered with red. Cliff crouched to leap back down to get one of the guns, and hesitated just a moment to gauge his distance. In that moment the gray dog slipped. The broken foreleg failed and the dog went skidding downward, dragging at the loose mud until he stopped, much closer to the creek and Eddie again, but glaring upward.

Now Cliff didn't dare to try getting down past him. He wouldn't have enough moments at the creek. He knew he had to cling and wait till the dog—those eyes and teeth—got up close to him again before a quick leap sideways could give him another lead. The dog started up toward him.

"Eddie!" he screamed. "Load the gun! Load the gun!"

Eddie still looked like he was in shock, but suddenly he moved. Cliff saw him jam the carbine downward, clamping it between his legs. Then the scrambling dog was right beneath him and Cliff clawed away across the slope, digging his way upward a bit.

He looked back down. "Eddie! Hurry!" He saw Eddie hunched up, one arm still limp, the other working busily trying to load the carbine. Cliff heard the snarling get louder and scrambled to the side, then fought his way upward again, the big teeth and glaring eyes less than ten feet from him. He was in a chase he couldn't keep winning. It wasn't a game; he needed a gun! This time he leaped without pausing; he sprang off from the side of the hill, kicked out his legs, and dropped back onto the slope on the side of one hip. Immediately he went into a controlled, swift slide straight back down into the icy water of the creek, hoping he was near the shotgun or that Eddie could throw him the carbine and shells.

He sprang up, grabbing a rock to defend himself and looking desperately around for the dog. But the dog hadn't followed him. He was high above, scrambling for the leafy forest edge at the top of the mud slope. Then a fierce explosion rang in Cliff's ears, and as he jumped he saw the dog jerk, then hunch up and seem to hang against the slope.

Cliff turned and saw Eddie near him, the carbine now jammed up against his shoulder, the barrel angling upward supported by just one hand, with one finger still squeezing hard on the trigger.

Then there was a movement above him as the dog came tumbling down, end over end, closer and closer, like a gray plummeting meteor. It struck heavily in the creek between them, making a thick splash, and lay in the water like a large, soft, and soggy mop.

Before the splash had settled, before either one of them could quit staring at the dog, they began to hear the muffled sounds of men shouting in the distance. Cliff felt too exhausted and shaky to call out an answer right away. And anyway, first he had to find the shotgun and reload it, and the carbine too, in case there were other dogs that would reach them before the men. Eddie simply sank down quietly on the muddy bank. He showed no pain from his bleeding arm, at least not yet, but he was starting to look pale and weak.

Men came noisily down through the woody brush.

"Hey! Anybody 'round?" a voice hollered clearly from straight along the creek toward the lake.

"This way," Cliff finally answered.

"There they are. Hurry up! There's kids hurt down here!"

Cliff watched them come splashing closer. He tried to answer questions and watch as they quickly laid Eddie down, wrapped him in their shirts, and hurriedly cleaned the torn arm and bound it to stop the bleeding. Cliff tried to show them that he wasn't hurt, that he could climb okay by himself back up to the pasture. He managed it, but his legs felt loose and wouldn't push nearly as hard as he tried to make them. He needed a boost to get over the tall fence.

Eddie's pa was just getting there with the other men and several vehicles. Cliff got into someone's station wagon and went speeding off to the hospital. The doctor could find nothing wrong with him except for some dirt-covered cuts and scrapes, a long strawberry on his hip from that last slide, and two slightly rubbery knees. Two nurses cleaned his cuts and Mom came to take him home. By then his knees had all their strength back.

Three days later, on Saturday evening, after the sheep were penned in the corrals for the night, he went back to the hospital with Mom and Dad to visit Eddie. There was a wad of bandages on Eddie's arm, and there were some important-looking jars and tubes and instruments on a table beside the bed, but everyone there seemed happy enough. That afternoon the lab result had come, reporting no trace of rabies in the big gray dog. Eddie could feel free of that danger.

"I guess they didn't find rabies in any of those dogs," Eddie's pa added.

"Good!" Cliff's dad said strongly. "That means Karla Dobley's free of it too."

"They say so," Eddie's pa agreed. "But there wouldn't have been a chance of knowing for sure if our kids hadn't stopped that gray one."

Dad nodded. He folded his arms and leaned against the doorway as he said, "Starved as those dogs were, they'd have gotten sick in some way pretty soon."

"What worries me now," said Eddie's ma from the chair by the window, "is what these two kids might try to tackle next."

"I hope it won't have to be anything like this again." Cliff's mom moved farther into the room, closer to Eddie. "How's your arm?" She smiled at him.

"Okay, I guess." Eddie grinned back. "I guess it's torn up a bit, but it's tougher than my neck would've been."

Eddie's ma also answered that question, but more solemnly and thankfully. "The doctor says it'll mend, though it might always be a little stiff. I tell him that's no worse'n me in damp weather."

"Me either," said Mom.

"But he'll have to do a lot of limbering exercises," Eddie's pa said with a wink, "like forking hay and getting up at two A.M. to check cows during calving."

It was meant as straight teasing, but Cliff knew

doing farm chores didn't bother Eddie a bit.

"What he needs," Cliff spoke up, "is to come to our place and practice swinging a fast bat. That'll straighten the arm out."

"Baseball!" Eddie groaned. Or was he laughing? It was hard to tell which. "Well—I've been thinking—maybe—I mean—well—" Eddie paused. "I mean, I was sure glad— You were sure handy winging those stones out there."

Coming from Eddie, such praise was surprising, even a little embarrassing. "Well," Cliff said, "it was you who knew how to find that dog. And *you* got him. You got *two* of them." But he couldn't just leave it like that. "Of course, I had to coach you on re-loading."

"So that's why you want me to come over. So you can keep rubbing that in."

"Not me," said Cliff. "I'd probably get confused and forget that too."

"I've been thinking of coming over." Eddie's voice lowered to a murmur, as if he weren't too sure of what he was about to say or of how Cliff would answer. "I guess baseball isn't all just a game."

"Sometimes it is," Cliff answered. It depends, he thought, on how serious you are. "Sometimes it's not," he said. "But you saved your throwing arm. I bet even with a sling on you can throw better than that hanging wire I've got out there. And maybe I can teach you to hit better than a rock wall."

Eddie's voice came bouncing back. "You'd better keep your mitt handy. If you throw 'em I'll hit 'em."

"If you can hit my throws one out of three I'll eat those balls!"

"That's a bet!" said Eddie.

"Shhh," said Mom. "We're in a hospital."

"Do you know what they're talking about?" asked Eddie's ma.

"Yes," said Dad. "But don't ask them to explain. I'll tell you later."

Maybe because of their loud voices a nurse came in. She rearranged a few things, then left, and the talk stayed quiet. Cliff moved closer to Eddie's bed and let their parents discuss things behind him, until somewhere in the hospital a clock hand moved and made a gong ring softly, telling them that visiting hours were over.

As they drove away from the hospital toward the sandy-gravel road home, they rode by the darkened park where the practices had already started and the season's games would soon begin being played.

"I take it you still wish you could play there," Dad said.

"I'll play there," Cliff answered. "As soon as I can drive in."

"I've been trying, and Mom too," Dad said, "to figure out how to get you in and out to practice this summer. But I can't let go of my job, and if Mom quits hers we're going to run short of cash later on. And there's no one out our way who just naturally drives back and forth to town at practice times."

"You'll still be home on weekends, won't you?" said Cliff.

"I sure plan to."

"Well, with you shagging with me then, and Eddie coming over three or four days during the week—"

"Eddie's going to have to be careful of his arm," said Mom.

"He can just hop around and get me used to playing with a runner on base," said Cliff. "Even if he just stands and hits easy lobs one-handed, I can use regular balls and get more throws in."

"Eddie may not want a steady job like that," said Dad.

"He's going to need help with his own chores and ideas. I'm going to go over there part of those days. We figured it out after that nurse left."

"But are you sure you want to get tied down to Eddie's kind of chores?" Dad asked seriously.

"They never hurt him," said Cliff.

"Will you have time?" said Mom.

"Well"—Cliff took a breath—"if we can put off

building any more pasture fence this summer, we'll save money not buying any more wire for a year."

"Wow!" Dad laughed. "You're not going to be just a player. You're going to be a manager too."

"With you and Eddie helping me," Cliff said, "I can do it on my own."

Then he sank down in the seat, as if he were drowsy, so as not to draw any more talk. "I'll show them," he told himself. "When the time comes, when the heat's on, I bet I keep my head. And by then I'll be able to throw even better."

Then for rest of the ride he pretended Mom's car was a taxi taking him out to the stadium to play in his first World Series.

ABOUT THE AUTHOR

Peter Zachary Cohen was born in Buffalo, New York, and grew up in both urban and rural New York State. After graduating from high school he moved west, and received his B.A. and M.S. degrees from the University of Wyoming.

Since 1961 Mr. Cohen has taught English at Kansas State University. He lives near Alta Vista, Kansas, with his wife, Suzanne, and their two sons, Todd and Jay, on one hundred acres of farm land where they raise crossbred sheep.